HAPPY MOTHER'S DAY

by STEVEN KROLL

illustrated by MARYLIN HAFNER

BRIGGS ST.

HOLIDAY HOUSE   NEW YORK

To my mother, who else?

Text copyright © 1985 by Steven Kroll
Illustrations copyright © 1985 by Marylin Hafner
All rights reserved
Printed in the United States of America

Library of Congress Cataloging in Publication Data

Kroll, Steven.
Happy Mother's Day

SUMMARY: One day when Mom returns home she is
greeted by surprise after surprise from each of her
six children and her husband.
   [1. Mother's Day—Fiction]   I. Hafner, Marylin,
ill.   II. Title.
PZ7.K9225Hap 1984   [E]   83-18498
ISBN 0-8234-0504-4

One day, when Mom got home, there was a note on the front door.

Mom dashed inside, threw off her coat, and ran upstairs to her bedroom. On the table beside the bed was a glass of milk and a plate of cookies. Beside the milk and cookies was a note.

"How very nice," Mom said out loud. "What a lovely surprise."

She quickly drank the milk and ate the cookies. Then she peeked under the bed.

"Surprise!" yelled Lenny, crawling out with a bouquet of daisies.

"Why Lenny," Mom said, "what pretty flowers."
"Now you have to come with me," said Lenny.
"There's another surprise."
"There is?" said Mom.

She followed Lenny across the hall into Linda's room. It was all cleaned up. It hadn't looked so clean since before last Christmas.

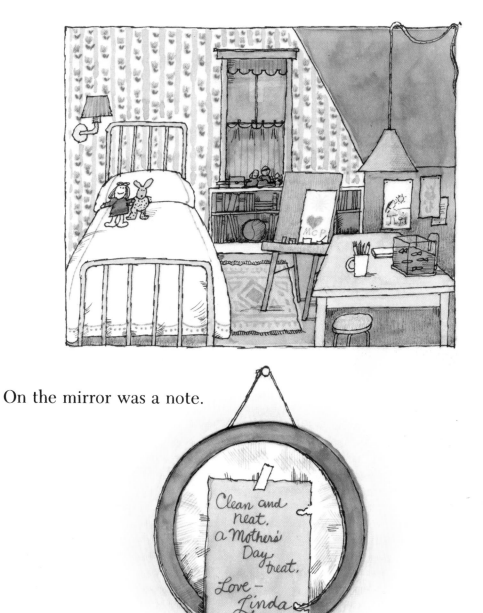

On the mirror was a note.

Clean and
neat,
a Mother's
Day
treat.

Love —
Linda

"My goodness," said Mom, "I can't believe this."
The closet door flew open. "Surprise!" Linda
shouted. And she held out a necklace of gold beads
she had made at school.

Mom put on the necklace. It sparkled.
"Thank you, Linda, it's lovely," she said.

Mom followed Linda and Lenny next door into Laurie's room. The windows that had needed washing for so long were spotless. On one of them was a note.

When dirt
is gone,
your day is
Bright.
Love,
Laurie

"Surprise!" Laurie shouted, jumping out from under her desk.

She held out a special bracelet she had made.

"I love it," said Mom, and gave Laurie a kiss.

"Now you have to come with me," said Laurie.

Mom followed Linda, Laurie and Lenny into Louise's room.

The torn curtains near the bed were mended. On the bed was a note.

"Well, that's just wonderful," said Mom.

Louise crawled out from behind a chair. "Surprise!" she shouted, and held out a long blue scarf.

The scarf went perfectly with the necklace and bracelet.

"I'm starting to feel like a queen," said Mom.

"You are a queen," said Lenny, Linda, Laurie, and Louise.

"Now you have to come with me," said Louise. "There's another surprise."

Mom followed Louise, Laurie, Linda, and Lenny down the stairs to the living room.

The table that had stood on three legs for so long now stood on four.

The fireplace that had been overflowing with ashes was clean.

On the mantel was a note.

The draperies flew apart. "Surprise!" said Larry.
"Why Larry," said Mom, "you got a haircut."
"I knew you'd be pleased," said Larry.
"You look wonderful," said Mom.
"Thanks," said Larry. "Now you have to come with me."

There's ANOTHER SurPrise!

Mom followed

Larry, Louise, Laurie, Linda, and Lenny

up to baby Lester's room.

Baby Lester was already in his pajamas.

On his crib was a note.

Dad got me
    ready for bed.
He did a very
    good job. Now you
have to come with
me. There's another
SURPRISE.

    xxx
    Lester

Larry picked up Lester, and Mom followed Lester, Larry, Louise, Laurie, Linda, and Lenny into the bathroom.

It was a tight squeeze.

The bathroom had been painted yellow.
On the mirror was a note.

Lenny pulled back the shower curtain. Dad was squashed into the bathtub. A big package was on his knees.

"Surprise!" he shouted.
He climbed out and kissed Mom.
"David," said Mom, "did you arrange all this?"
"Nope," said Dad. "It was a group effort."
Mom smiled at everyone and opened the package.

Inside was a hat

with a broad brim

and a feather.

She put it on.

"Now you have to come with me," said Dad. "There's another surprise!"

"You mean there's more?"

"Just one more thing."

Mom followed Dad, Larry, baby Lester, Louise, Laurie, Linda, and Lenny into the dining room.

Dinner was ready and waiting, and in the middle
of the table was a huge cake.

Written across the icing was:

Mom hugged everyone.
She said, "You've all done so much.

This is the nicest thing that
has ever happened to me."

And Dad, baby Lester,

Larry,

Louise,

Linda,

Laurie,

and Lenny replied,

"You're the nicest thing that has ever happened to us!"

And they all sat down to celebrate together.

Kroll, Steven
Happy Mother's Day

JJ
S

HOLIDAY

DATE DUE

JE 01 07			
MY 27 '08			
MY 2 0 09			
MY 26 '10			
MY 2 6 '11			
MMY 2 9 213			
MY 1 9 '15			